Victoria Harwood

THREE SHORT
ADVENTURE
STORIES
BOOK 2

Collection of
"One Hundred Bedtime Stories"

This book is a wonderful collection of short stories
perfect for young children.
Each story covers a **different** theme, such as kindness,
friendship, discovery, love, and the diversity of living
creatures in both our world and imaginary ones. It's an
ideal choice for bedtime reading or for young readers
who are just starting to explore the joys of literature.

The Model Ship

Our neighbours, an old couple, live in the house next to us. Their daughter often visits them with her son, Oliver, their grandson. Sitting in the garden, we hear adults constantly shout his name as if scolding him.

Oliver is a brilliant, resourceful, but slightly naughty boy, and he can't sit still. He reminded me of another Oliver, who is now an adult. I knew him as a boy in my childhood, and sometimes we played together with other friends.

My friend Oliver was also a restless boy who was constantly busy making things.

His favourite activity was to make paper boats and try to float them in the nearby stream to see how far they would go.

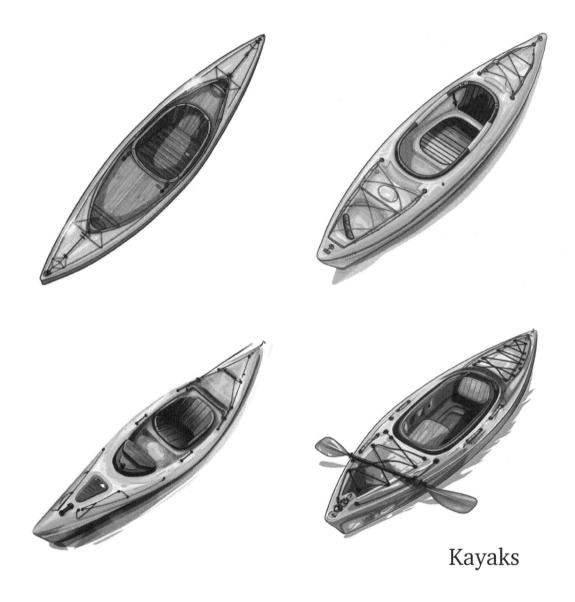

Kayaks

He was getting more and more adventurous with his boats. He made many types: longboats, single and double-tube steamers, narrow boats, kayaks, sailboats and rafts.

Oliver seemed to have a vast knowledge of all types of water vessels and what they were called and used for. Many of them I had never even heard of, and Oliver patiently listed them to me:

Container ship

"Container ships for the transport of containers. Bulk carriers for the transport of dry cargo. Lumber carriers carry timber, and tankers carry oil. Passenger ships - this is understandable for the transport of passengers.

Trawlers for catching fish.

And using ferries, you can cross wide rivers or get to an island by sea from the mainland."

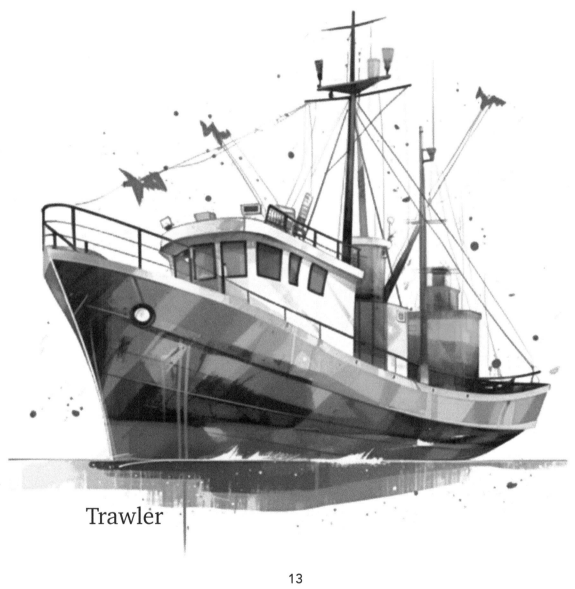

Trawler

Steamship

Destoryer

15

Oliver knew how a kayak differed from a canoe, a cutter from a motorboat, and a steamboat from a schooner. He could also describe in great detail what a gondola looked like.

Oliver and his dad made models of a particular group of ships – ones that had sails, both modern and old. They were all known by interesting names.

Canoe boat

Drakkar

Viking Drakkar is a long boat with a sail.

Frigates and Galleys, Caravels and sailing Barges.

From him, I learned that there are single-masted, two-masted and three-masted ships and what a mast is.

Do you know what a mast is on a sailing ship?

Yes, it is a tall pole on which the sails are attached, and they can be controlled with cables and winches.

Single-masted ships: Egyptian papyrus boat, Gunboat, Drakkar, Sloop.

Two-masted: Brig, Brigantine, Schooner, Galley.

Three-masted: Barque, Galleon, Caravel, Clipper, Corvette.

Frigate

Brigantine

Caravel

Oliver dreamed of becoming a captain or first mate. He could talk about ships and navigation for hours, but everyone listened to him only briefly as we all preferred to do something practical with boats in the nearby stream.

Oliver taught us all how to make boats out of a sheet of paper. We would then launch them into the water for a race and run screaming along the riverbank, each supporting our creation.

We also had much fun putting obstacles and dams in the shallow stream for them to see how the boats managed to manoeuvre between them as if by magic.

Sailing Yacht

Oliver also said he sailed with his grandfather's real yacht and showed how to handle the sails. All of his stories were incredible. But I saw with my own eyes how many models of different ships they had in their house and even met his grandfather.

The whole family went to the sea for the summer; only their mother and Oliver stayed home until the school holidays began.

One day, Oliver did not go out into the garden, although it was warm and sunny. I shouted to Oliver, but his mother came out and told us he had a cold and was unwell. It was a bit boring without Oliver. We decided to visit him at home, and his mother said we could see him in the house. The three of us went inside.

In the house, everything looked exceptional. Each room had a wall that was covered entirely with shelves. On each of them were models of ships from different times, boats made of plastic and wood, with and without sails.

On the wall in the living room hung a real steering wheel from an old ship. We had come to see Oliver, but it was difficult to tear ourselves away from this vast display. We eventually found our way to our friend's bedroom.

He lay in bed and was enthusiastically crafting something out of paper. We were glad to see him sitting up. Oliver put down his creation and smiled.

"You see, I caught a cold, but not a usual winter one."

He then began to tell us exactly what had happened to him.

Oliver had assembled a model sailboat all alone, which was radio-controlled. He decided to go and launch it by himself and not wait for his dad to go with him.

Oliver carefully tied the box with the model to the pannier of his bicycle and went to the sea, which was three miles from our house. He was eager to test the model and see how it would float—the day promised to be sunny. The boy stopped at a small concrete pier on the sandy shore and unpacked the model.

The propeller of the sailboat was powered by a battery built into the ship's hull.

Oliver did not notice the approaching storm clouds and the waves that were gradually becoming larger and larger. The sun hid as if it did not approve of the boy's activity. Oliver was singularly fascinated with how the sailboat behaved and did not notice anything else around him.

At one moment, the wind blew stronger, raised a large wave, and the sailboat began to be carried away to the open sea. It was no longer obeying his command.

The boy was in despair. He collected and glued this model for six months, and now it seemed that everything was over. But Oliver could just about see the top of the mast and the sailboat bravely fighting the waves.

Without hesitation, Oliver got into a small boat that was parked against the pier with one oar inside and decided to go and save his sailboat.

We looked at Oliver with admiration; how brave he seemed to us! But is it courage? Adults would call it recklessness.

The waves rocked the boat, which was challenging to manage with only one oar in such windy weather. Oliver remembered everything his grandfather had taught him.

He tried not to let the sailboat out of sight and rowed with all his might towards it. It then began to rain, and Oliver could not catch up with his sailboat. It was still afloat, but the waves carried it farther and farther from the land.

Luckily, at some point, a fisherman on the shore saw the boat with the boy and called the rescue station. From there, a red rescue boat quickly set off with a team of three lifeguards.

Oliver was by now very wet and tired of fighting the waves and did not know how to return to his bike.

He rowed courageously with a single oar, turning the boat around and preventing it from capsizing, as his grandfather had taught him. Rescuers arrived in time and transferred the boy into their boat, and the other boat was taken in tow. Everyone returned safely to shore.

"Yes, everything is fine," - Oliver smiled - "my mother hardly scolded me, but for some reason, she looked at me very sadly". His grandfather said that although he acted stupidly, he was proud he had learned what he had been taught. Dad didn't say anything and still avoids talking about it. I hope he will forgive me.

We all breathed a sigh of relief. At that moment, the doorbell rang, so we decided it was time to leave.

Then, his mother came into the room with a man wearing a bright orange jacket, and they both were smiling. We stepped aside, and the lifeguard placed a sailboat on Oliver's bed, his sailboat.

"I don't believe it, this cannot be," exclaimed Oliver, carefully hugged the boat, and began to cry. "Thank you very much; I didn't even expect to see it again!" - he lovingly held the boat in his hands and tried to straighten the torn sails.

"Your sailboat is also a hero; it managed to survive in such weather," said the rescuer and smiled; "I hope you got a good lesson that you can't joke with the sea," he saluted cheerfully and left.

Mother said the sailboat had washed ashore from the lifeguard station. Since the locals knew that a boy had recently been rescued there on a boat, they brought the sailboat to the rescuers in the hope that they would return it to the boy.

Oliver soon recovered, and we all played together again and launched paper boats in the local stream.

As an adult, Oliver became a maritime pilot; he worked on a boat that guided large ships between the open sea and the docks.

I think his dream came true!

Three Short Adventure Stories

Ecounter with a Bear

with

a Bear

Daniel's grandfather lived in Alaska. His house stood on the edge of a pine forest in a small village near a fast river that rushed down from the top of the mountains that overlooked it.

It was a wonderful place with air that had a remarkable freshness. You could feel the power of life in everything. Life in a forest in Alaska was only for strong-willed people; his grandfather liked to remind him now and again.

Usually, they visited their grandfather in the summer, which didn't last long in this region.

During this short time, all nature rushed to endow everyone living there with its riches: pine nuts, forest berries, mushrooms, fish, fresh herbs and, of course, its clean air.

Outside of summer, time is taken up with a long, snowy winter when you can ski on snow, crisp from frost, or stay home in the warmth. Daniel was with his grandfather only once during winter and liked it.

The boy loved to listen to his grandfather's stories about his adventures in the forest.

His trips with friends, encounters with wild animals, fishing and hunting. These sounded like real adventures to the boy, so he constantly asked his grandfather to take him to one day. Daniel was only eight years old, and his mother was against it. She was worried that he would get tired, mosquitoes would bite him, and, in general, such walks in the wild forest were not for children.

On one of these summer stays, when the weather was looking its best, they both managed to persuade Mother to let them go for a three-day trip through the forest.

Only he and his grandfather went on this journey.

Dad was busy with his affairs. Daniel felt like an adult and helped his grandfather pack as best he could. He was a scout cub and remembered what kind of things were required for a stay in a forest. Grandfather just nodded, surprised that he knew so much. Mother suggested packing three sweaters and a warm jacket. Dad pointed out that three were too many, explaining that they would spend one night in the hunter's hut with a fire stove, and the summer nights were not so cold anyway.

Grandfather said that after leaving the hut, they would take a boat down the river to get to the deep forest.

It was necessary to take a supply of food, dishes, a small axe to chop wood, a fishing rod to catch fish, cereals, mosquito spray and a few other useful things. After all the preparations, they had two backpacks, a small tent and sleeping bags. Of course, Daniel took with him an album and pencils to make sketches. Dad gave his son strict instructions to obey his grandfather at all times and never ever step far away from him. He explained that in the forest, one must always be alert; this is a wild world with its own laws.

The hike to the hut was very interesting. Grandfather talked a lot about life in the forest and showed useful plants, edible mushrooms, and berries – wild raspberries,

bilberries and cranberries. They found traces of wild animals, and the grandfather taught the boy to recognise birds by their songs. They slept in a real log cabin the first night. It was a low wooden one-room place with a small window. It isn't easy to notice such a hut in the forest; its roof is covered with turf and grass. Inside, there was a stove and a stove bench. It smelled of wood, pine needles, and adventure. The boy loved everything!

They made a fire in the stove, and grandfather fried the fish they had caught for dinner, cooked porridge and drank compote from wild berries.

Never before had Daniel eaten porridge better than this.

The boy did not have time to sketch everything that he wanted to draw, so he took a lot of photographs in order that he could make drawings from them later. He saw how beautiful a stone was covered with moss, noticed beauty even in a tree broken by the wind, and fog seemed to float over the river in the morning.

On the second day, he and his grandfather got into a boat and sailed down the river for a long time along the forest banks, bending around large stones in the water.

Grandfather told Daniel that due to the negligence of a person after a campfire, the forest often burns, and then it takes a very long time for it to recover.

They came out of the river to examine such a place where, instead of trees, black sticks and only low bushes covered everything around. They found plenty of blueberries and lingonberries here. This place had an extraordinary feeling, as the birds and animals left it to escape from the fire a few years ago. Daniel took some photos. Everything around looked sad.

The boy wished this forest would recover and become a home for many living creatures again. They returned to the boat and continued their journey down the river towards their overnight camp.

The second night, they had to sleep in a tent. Daniel sat by the fire with his grandfather for a long time and admired the starry sky. He enjoyed this moment so much but tried not to show that he was a bit afraid. Something constantly creaked in the dark bushes, and an owl hooted in the distance. Grandfather said that he would sit by the fire, and Daniel could go to sleep in a tent. They are in the forest near the river, and it is very important to keep the fire going to scare the wild animals away from their camp.

The boy obeyed and climbed into the tent to sleep. He was very tired during the day from many impressions and fell asleep quickly.

The night was quiet and moonlit. Grandfather was dozing by the fire. Somewhere near the river, the frogs sang loudly. The forest never sleeps; rustles are heard all the time.

The boy was awakened by a loud cracking of branches right next to the tent and his grandfather's loud shout. It was a bear who was attracted by the smells of cooked food and had decided to check if it was possible to get an easy morsel. At this time of the year, the bears are not hungry and would not be very dangerous, but you should not joke with them; it is better to try to drive them away.

Grandfather shouted:

"Daniel, in the boat, quickly!"

Grandfather stood in front of a huge bear and waved a long burning log, attempting to drive away the uninvited guest. The boy grabbed his backpack, got out of the tent and ran to the boat. From there, he could see the open mouth of a bear, standing upright and grandfather with his burning stick in his hand. He shouted and lunged towards the beast, trying to set fire to its fur. Apparently, the bear was not hungry as it recoiled and ran away.

The boy was sitting in the boat, shivering from the morning cold, and looked at his grandfather admiringly, who hastily collected the tent and dishes. Soon, they rowed away from the shore so as not to risk another encounter should the bear return.

The grandfather looked at his grandson and praised him for the speed with which he followed his instructions.

"The forest is a wild world; you must always be ready to react quickly and decide how best to escape if danger is close. Well done!" he said.

And Daniel remembered the wild beast for a long time. It was a dangerous and magnificent sight. He was determined to become as strong and brave as his grandfather.

The boy was relieved that the rest of the journey had passed without any further incidents, but he was happy to have taken this memorable trip.

The boy had listened attentively to his grandfather's stories along the way and understood that he had a lot to learn.

At home, both of them talked excitedly about their meeting with the bear. Mum and Dad looked at them like heroes and were very glad they managed to escape such a difficult situation without injury.

"All's well that ends well," Dad said, "next time I will join you; it seems I missed an adventure."

The boy grew up and became an artist and a wildlife photographer.

He painted a picture called "Incident in the Forest" and presented it to his grandfather on his eightieth birthday.

Life is like a book of stories, unforgettable moments that we create, and events that happen to us. Everyone has this book, and I'm sure you already have many interesting pages in your book already!

The Girl
and the
Sea

There was once a girl who loved the sea very much: swimming near the beach, watching it from afar in stormy weather, snorkeling and marveling at the underwater world, playing with the waves, running on the sand. Sometimes, simply sitting by the water, breathing the sea air, and watching the noisy seagulls overhead.

The girl visited the sea several times with her parents. On the days she was not there, she imagined how she would come and say – "Hello, here I am!"

This girl loved the sea so much she often dreamed about it.

She dreamed of the salty sea spray being blown from the top of the waves, their unique sound and their very beautiful greenish colour.

White sand and a scattering of small shells, fast fish flashing underwater, funny crabs with eyes on stilts and large claws. These dreams filled the girl with joy and a good mood for the whole day. The sea was her friend. A friend with whom she wanted to talk or be silent or play with.

The girl did not know how big the sea was. She felt that it is a living being, it hears and understands her.

One day, Dad bought the girl a snorkelling mask and showed her how to breathe through a tube underwater. The girl learned to hold her breath and observe life underwater. It was beautiful and a completely different world! A unique magical world of the underwater kingdom of fish and dolphins, whales and sea anemones, octopuses and many other living creatures appeared before her...

Mum and Dad did not often allow her to swim far, but there were many exciting things near the shore.

Here, a crustacean has made its home in a twisted shell and wears it everywhere like a comfortable coat. If you get too close, then he hides inside it. One day, the girl met a baby octopus as it swam. They both saw each other, got scared and froze, and then began to play, swimming in a circle. The little octopus even allowed itself to be touched.

The girl loved to watch how quickly shrimps burrow into the sand and how funny they swim, twisting their tail in a circle.

Small anemones stick to fingers; self-important jellyfish do not like to be touched. Fishes are always curious and swim close to the girl to say hello but are often too busy looking for food.

Yes, the girl had many reasons to love the sea, and the sea loved the girl. In the mornings, it runs up to her feet in waves, greets her, inviting her to play and laugh together as if it is in a good mood.

When the sea is not angry, it is very kind; it glitters and sparkles in the sun with its waves and splashes. It seems that nothing can be more beautiful than this.

One day, the girl's father went off in a boat to fish. In the morning, the day was sunny, and the sky was clear, but suddenly, it turned dark purple. A storm appeared out of nowhere. Huge waves crashed against the pier and over the sand.

The girl did not know why the sea was sometimes angry. She worried about her dad and waited on the shore for him to return. A cool wind doused it with sea spray and raised high waves, throwing jellyfish and small fishes ashore that did not have time to escape. Heavy rain with gusts of wind wet the girl's dress and hair.

But she still walks along the shore and talks to the sea.

She tells the sea her thoughts out loud:

- All bad things pass, and there is no need to be so angry. An agitated sea is not as beautiful as a calm one. Many creatures who are unable to cope with the waves are in trouble. She loves her dad very much.

The girl was small, but the sea was vast and formidable in its rage.

She entered the sea knee-deep and held out her hands to it.

- Oh, the sea, you are my friend! Help my dad get back to the shore! You are strong and mighty; you can do so much! I love you, my sea! Please calm down a little. I don't know what makes you so angry, but everything comes to an end, and so there is no need to worry!

The girl was very sure that the sea heard her because it quietly calmed down. The wind became gentler, and a sunbeam cut through the veil of low, dark thunderclouds.

- Thank you! - the girl shouted, - Thank you, my dear sea!

She threw her favourite ring into the foamy waves. The sea sobbed with a splash, and smiles sparkled in the sunbeams.

The girl ran to the pier. She saw a boat and her tired Dad full of stories of his adventure and rescue.

The girl turned to the sea and waved. Then she took her father by the hand, and they returned home.

Thank you!

Thank you for reading our kind stories.

There is some truth in every fairytale!

Be brave, read more interesting stories and fairytales and magical doors to other adventures will start opening for you.

Special thanks

Special thanks to Igor Kirko and Zinaida Kirko for the practical advice and support in creating the book and illustrations.

My thanks also to Leslie Harwood, an excellent translator and kind editor.

Published books of
our project:

W712

DREAM WORLD

Zinaida Kirko

Dragon Island

Zinaida Kirko

Jackie's Adventures in the World of Letters

About Anything and Everything

Book 1 from the series of books for children "One Hundred Bedtime Stories"

About Everything and Anything

Book 2 from the series of books for children "One Hundred Bedtime Stories"

The Isle called Ploof

and other inhabitants of the ocean

TRUE FRIENDS

92

WELCOME TO
THE HAPPY STORY GARDEN

https://thehappystorygarden.co.uk

Milton Keynes UK
Ingram Content Group UK Ltd.
UKHW051421030424
440540UK00005BA/18